PONY PALS

Ponies from the Past

Jeanne Be[...]

Illustrate[...] y Paul Bachem

A
LITTLE APPLE
PAPERBACK

SCHOLASTIC INC.

New York   Toronto   London   Auckland   Sydney
Mexico City   New Delhi   Hong Kong   Buenos Aires

The author thanks Liz Shapiro, Director of the Sharon Historical Society; Linda Wasley, Sharon Town Clerk; and Diane Hernsdors, Director of the Hartford Medical Society for applying their knowledge of the past to this story.

ISBN 0-439-21640-0

Copyright © 2001 by Jeanne Betancourt.
All rights reserved. Published by Scholastic Inc.

SCHOLASTIC, LITTLE APPLE PAPERBACKS, and associated logos are trademarks and/or registered trademarks of Scholastic Inc.

12 11 10 9 8 7 6 5 4 3 2 1   1 2 3 4 5 6/0

Printed in the U.S.A.
First Scholastic printing, July 2001

Contents

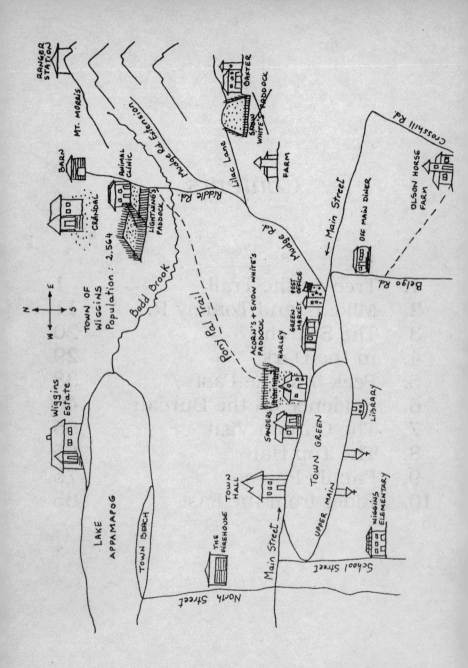

Tree on the Trail

Lulu Sanders galloped her pony, Snow White, along Pony Pal Trail. Anna Harley followed on her brown-and-black Shetland pony, Acorn. Anna and Lulu were meeting their Pony Pal, Pam Crandal. Pony Pal Trail was a mile-and-a-half trail through the woods. It went from Snow White and Acorn's paddock to the Crandals' big field.

Lulu noticed that a tree had fallen across the trail. I rode here yesterday, thought Lulu. There weren't any trees blocking my way. That tree must have fallen during the storm last night. Lulu slowed Snow White to a walk.

"A tree fell across the trail ahead," Lulu called back to Anna.

"Can we jump it?" asked Anna.

"Yes," answered Lulu. "It's an easy jump and the ground on the other side is smooth."

Lulu moved Snow White into a trot, leaned forward in the saddle, and gave her the signal to jump. But Snow White didn't jump. Instead she stopped in front of the fallen tree.

"It's just an old tree," Lulu told Snow White. "You've jumped over them before."

Snow White lowered her head and sniffed at the tree.

Lulu dismounted. "All right," she said. "You can walk around it. But jumping would have been easier."

Snow White whinnied softly and nodded. Lulu finally saw what had caught Snow White's attention. A glass jar lay beside the tree trunk.

Anna and Acorn rode up to them. "I thought we were going to jump," said Anna.

"Snow White found a jar," Lulu told her as she bent over and picked it up.

"I hate it when people leave their trash on the trails," said Anna.

"It's an old jar," said Lulu. "I think it's been here for a long time."

Anna dismounted to have a closer look.

Lulu brushed some tree rot off the jar. "It has one of those glass tops with a metal clamp," she observed.

"My grandmother used to can tomatoes in jars like that," said Anna.

"The metal's all rusted," Lulu pointed out. "And there's an envelope inside."

"Open the jar," said Anna excitedly. "I want to see what's in the envelope."

"Let's do it at Pam's," suggested Lulu. "We can look at it together."

"Good idea," agreed Anna.

Lulu put the jar in her saddlebag. The two girls walked their ponies around the fallen

tree and galloped the rest of the way to Pam's. They couldn't wait to open the jar.

Pam was saddling up her pony, Lightning, when Anna and Lulu arrived.

"Look what we found," said Lulu as she jumped off Snow White. Anna told Pam all about the fallen tree and finding the jar. Lulu handed the jar to Pam.

"Open it," said Anna. "I bet there's a letter inside."

Pam scowled.

"What's wrong?" asked Lulu.

"We shouldn't read someone else's mail," answered Pam.

"It's a very *old* jar," explained Lulu. "I think it's been in the woods for a long, long time."

"It's like a message from the past," said Anna. "It's okay for us to read it."

"It might be a mystery for us to solve," added Lulu. "A Pony Pal mystery."

"Okay," agreed Pam reluctantly. She handed the jar back to Lulu. "You open it."

Lulu pulled on the rusty metal clamp. It didn't move. She put her thumbs under the clamp and pushed. Finally, the clamp released. Lulu took off the glass lid and handed the jar to Anna.

"You found the jar, so you take out the letter," Anna told Lulu.

"Actually, Snow White found it," said Lulu. "I'll take it out for her."

Lulu pulled the envelope out of the jar and unrolled it. The envelope was brittle and yellow. *LS* was written on the front in faded black ink. Lulu turned the envelope over. It was sealed with blue wax.

"It looks so *old*," said Pam.

"Open it," whispered Anna. "Break the seal."

Lulu pried the wax with her fingernail. The dried-out wax crumbled. Lulu's heart pounded.

Lulu opened the envelope and pulled out a folded piece of paper. She unfolded it and held it out for Anna and Pam to see. Pam took the letter and read it out loud.

October 18, 1918

Dear L S

John said he would leave this letter for you in the tree. I miss you and Bangles so much. I am very weak. I sleep a lot. For a short while each day, I sit by the Window. From there I can see Wildflower in her paddock. I wish you could come visit. That would be the best medicine for me. Sometimes I'm afraid that I will never again be healthy.

I hope that Mike doesn't have the influenza. He is such a darling baby. I am praying for him.

I made John promise not to tell George O. and Edwin P. about our hiding place for letters. Even John doesn't know about our secret riding field, where girls and ponies are free. Give Bangles a kiss for me.

Your best friend forever,
A W

Postscript
Write back as soon as possible. John will check the tree tomorrow and bring me the jar. I keep all the letters you write to me in the bottom of my sewing basket.

Pam finished reading the letter.

"Wow!" exclaimed Anna. "Nineteen eighteen is a long time ago."

"The letter was in that tree for all those years!" said Lulu.

"I wonder who LS and AW were," said Pam.

"They had ponies," said Lulu. "Wildflower and Bangles."

"AW is a girl," said Lulu.

"How do you know?" asked Anna. "A could be for Andrew, Anthony, Alan, or Andy. There are a lot of boys' names that begin with A."

"AW had a sewing basket," answered Lulu. "That was a girl thing."

"I bet LS was a girl, too," said Pam.

"And those two boys — George O. and Edwin P. — pestered them a lot," added Anna.

"Just like Mike and Tommy pester us," said Lulu.

"The girls had a special place where they liked to ride," Anna said. "A secret place."

"A place where they felt free," said Pam.

"Free from teasing boys," added Anna.

"AW was sick when she wrote the letter," observed Pam.

"She was *very* sick," said Lulu. "She was afraid she would never get better."

"I wonder if she did," said Pam sadly.

Lulu carefully folded the letter and put it in the envelope. "I want to know who those two girls were," she said. "And what happened to them."

"Let's go to the tree," said Pam. She tightened Lightning's girth. "I want to see where you found the letter."

"Maybe we'll find more clues," said Lulu.

"Like more jars with letters in them," Anna said.

Lulu put the jar back in her saddlebag and swung up on Snow White. She led the way back to Pony Pal Trail. As she rode she thought about the letter.

AW wrote a letter to LS in 1918. John put it in a tree for LS to find. The tree was a secret hiding place. When the Pony Pals opened the jar, the letter was still closed with a wax seal. LS never read the letter that AW wrote to her. Why not? wondered Lulu.

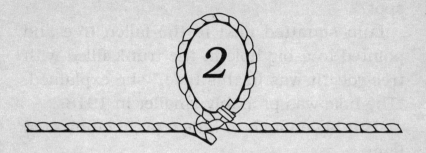

Mike L. and Tommy R.

The girls rode their ponies to the fallen tree and walked all around it.

Anna stood next to the tree's broken roots. "It was on Ms. Wiggins's land," she observed.

Ms. Wiggins was a good friend of the Pony Pals. She had a lot of land with great riding trails. The Pony Pals could ride there whenever they wanted.

The three girls carefully checked inside and around the tree for more jars and other clues. They didn't find any.

"Where did Snow White find the jar?"

asked Pam. "Do you remember the exact spot?"

Lulu squatted next to the fallen tree and pointed to a big hole in the trunk filled with tree rot. "It was in this hole," she explained. "The hole was probably smaller in 1918."

"But big enough to hide a jar," commented Pam.

"I'll show you what I think happened," said Lulu. She put the jar in the tree trunk. "The jar was in the hole. When the tree fell, the jar rolled out." Lulu gave the jar a little push. It rolled out of the tree and onto the ground.

"The jar had some tree rot on it," Anna told Pam. "That's more evidence that it was in the tree."

Lulu put the jar back in the tree. "It was put there on October 18, 1918," she said. "That's over — "

"Shh," warned Pam. "Someone's coming."

Lulu heard voices. She looked into the woods. "It's Tommy and Mike," she whispered. "On their bikes."

Just then Tommy Rand and Mike Lacey

saw the girls. "It's the Pony Pests," shouted Tommy.

"Quick. Hide the jar," Pam whispered to Lulu.

Lulu sat down on the tree trunk so that her backside covered the hole.

Mike and Tommy rode up to the girls.

"How are your little ponies today?" asked Tommy. "Are the little girls and their little ponies playing in the woods?"

"Leave us alone, Tommy," said Pam.

"I'm sure you have something better to do," added Lulu. "Or maybe you don't."

"I'm working for Ms. Wiggins," said Mike. "I'm checking her woods for trees that fell in the storm." He looked at the fallen tree. "But this one wasn't on her land."

"Yes it was," Anna told him. She pointed to where the tree had grown. "See?"

"Oh, yeah," agreed Mike. He took out a notebook and wrote something down. "A lot of trees fell during the storm last night," Mike told Anna. "That's the fifth one I've found."

"What are you telling *her* for?" Tommy asked Mike.

"I was — ah — just writing it down," answered Mike. He looked embarrassed and a little afraid of Tommy. Lulu hated when Tommy bullied Mike. She also hated that Mike let Tommy bully him.

"Get up," Mike ordered Lulu. "I have to look at the whole tree."

"You can't tell me what to do, Mike Lacey," said Lulu. She glanced quickly at Anna and thought, Distract Mike and Tommy so I can hide the jar.

Anna got the message. She gave Acorn a signal, and Acorn nudged Tommy in the back.

Tommy almost fell over. "Hey! Who did that?" he shouted angrily.

Next, Acorn nudged Mike. Mike looked a little frightened of Acorn and backed away.

Acorn is so great at doing tricks, thought Lulu. While Mike and Tommy weren't looking, she stood up and put the jar in her saddlebag.

"Get that dumb pony away from me!" Tommy yelled at Anna.

"He used to be your pony, Tommy Rand," Anna reminded him.

"You were in a parade on Acorn," added Pam.

"And you had on a teddy bear costume," said Anna. "Your mother showed us the picture. You were such a *cute* little boy."

"A teddy bear?" laughed Mike. "You were dressed like a *teddy bear*?"

Tommy glared at Mike. Mike stopped laughing. "Sorry," he mumbled.

"Hey, Mike, I thought you wanted to look at the tree," said Lulu as she mounted Snow White.

Pam and Anna mounted their ponies, too.

"Let's go," Anna said. "We've got better things to do than be insulted by Tommy the Teddy Bear and his sidekick, Mike."

As the Pony Pals rode off, the boys shouted insults at them. Good riddance, thought Lulu. She watched Pam and Anna riding ahead of her. How lucky I am to have

Pony Pals. Pam and Anna love the outdoors, ponies, and solving mysteries as much as I do.

Lulu Sanders had learned a lot about the outdoors and nature from her father. Mr. Sanders traveled all over the world to study wild animals. Lulu's mother died when Lulu was young. After that, Lulu had traveled with her father. But when Lulu turned ten, he decided it was time for Lulu to live in one place. Now Lulu lived with her grandmother in Wiggins. Lulu loved living in Wiggins, where she could have her own pony and be a Pony Pal.

Pam Crandal and Anna Harley had been best friends since kindergarten. Pam was tall and Anna was short. Pam liked school and got the best marks. Anna was dyslexic, so reading and writing were difficult for her. She didn't like school. But Anna was a terrific artist. Lulu loved Anna's drawings and paintings, especially the ones she did of ponies and horses.

The girls came to the end of Pony Pal Trail.

"Let's go to the diner," suggested Anna. "We can have a snack and a Pony Pal meeting about the letter."

The girls rode to Off-Main Diner and tied their ponies to the hitching post. Anna's mother owned the diner. It was a perfect place for Pony Pal meetings. Lulu carefully removed the letter from the jar and they went inside. They ordered brownies and milk and sat in their favorite booth.

Lulu opened the letter and they all read it again.

"The tree was on Ms. Wiggins's land," observed Lulu. "*W* could be the initial for Wiggins."

"Maybe AW was an ancestor of Ms. Wiggins," suggested Pam. "And she lived in the house Ms. Wiggins lives in now."

Lulu studied the drawing of the house with the girl in the window. "This isn't Ms. Wiggins's house," she said. "It's not big enough."

"Ms. Wiggins told me the house used to be smaller," said Anna. "It wasn't all built at once." She pointed to the drawing. "This is probably the original part of the house. The windows are the same."

"We'll have to ask Ms. Wiggins," said Pam. "We should show her the letter, anyway. It was on her land."

"Let's go there next," suggested Anna.

Lulu folded the letter and put it back in the envelope. "I hope Tommy and Mike aren't at Ms. Wiggins's," she said.

"Whatever happens," said Anna, "don't let Tommy and Mike know about the letter."

"We'll ask Ms. Wiggins to keep it a secret, too," said Lulu.

Lulu bit into a brownie. She wondered if Ms. Wiggins could help them with the mystery of the letter. Would she know who AW and LS were?

The Search

The Pony Pals rode into the big field behind Ms. Wiggins's barns. "There's Ms. Wiggins," said Anna. "She's painting."

Ms. Wiggins was standing at an easel on the other side of the field. She looked up and waved to the Pony Pals. They rode over to her.

"I'm about to take a break," said Ms. Wiggins. "Do you girls want to come in for a snack?"

"We just had one at the diner," said Pam. "Can we see your painting?"

"Sure," said Ms. Wiggins. "But it's not finished."

The three girls looked at the painting.

"It already looks beautiful," said Anna. Pam and Lulu agreed. They all thought Ms. Wiggins was an excellent artist.

"We have something to show you," said Anna. "Snow White found it. It was on your land."

Ms. Wiggins frowned. "I hope it isn't an animal trap," she said.

"Oh, no," said Anna.

"It's a mystery," said Pam.

Lulu told Ms. Wiggins about the fallen tree and how Snow White had found the jar. She showed Ms. Wiggins the letter. Ms. Wiggins read the letter carefully.

"How interesting," she said. "This drawing is of my house, you know. That's the way it used to look."

"That's what Anna said," Pam commented.

"It's definitely a drawing of the original house," said Ms. Wiggins. "AW must have lived here. She was a good artist like you, Anna."

"And like you," said Anna.

"Do you think the *W* stands for Wiggins?" asked Pam.

"It probably does," said Ms. Wiggins. "Now who was AW?" She thought for a few seconds. "I've got it!" she exclaimed. "*A* is for *Abigail.* My great-aunt Abigail Stevenson. My grandfather was John Wiggins, Abigail's brother. He must be the one who put the letter in the tree."

"AW can't be Abigail *Stevenson,*" said Pam disappointedly. "We're looking for *AW* not AS."

"Abigail married someone named Stevenson," explained Lulu. "But her name was Abigail Wiggins when she wrote the letter. Right?"

"Exactly," agreed Ms. Wiggins. "Abigail Wiggins lived in this house. I wonder why LS didn't read Abigail's letter."

"We were wondering about that, too," said Anna.

"Put your ponies in the paddock and meet me in the parlor," said Ms. Wiggins. "Mean-

while, I'll see what I can remember about Great-aunt Abigail. This is a fascinating mystery."

"If you see Mike," cautioned Lulu, "don't tell him about the letter. He and Tommy have been teasing us a lot."

"Just like George O. and Edwin P. teased Abigail and LS," Ms. Wiggins said with a smile.

"Exactly," said the Pony Pals together.

The girls took off their ponies' saddles and bridles and led them to the paddock. Ms. Wiggins's black horse, Picasso, and her pony, Beauty, were already there. Anna opened the paddock gate. Lulu patted Snow White's backside. "Go have fun with your pals," she said. The ponies and Picasso greeted one another with sniffs and nickers.

"I wonder if Bangles and Wildflower were ever together in this paddock," said Anna.

"I bet they were," said Lulu.

"Maybe their ghosts are still here," joked Pam.

"Maybe," said Anna. Lulu knew that Anna

wasn't joking. She took ghosts very seriously.

Ms. Wiggins was waiting for the girls in the parlor.

"Did you remember anything about Abigail Wiggins?" Lulu asked her.

"My great-aunt Abigail died when I was a girl," said Ms. Wiggins. "She was a very nice person. I remember that."

"Did she ever tell you stories about when she was a girl?" asked Anna. "Did she ever mention a pony named Wildflower?"

"Or talk about a best friend with the initials LS?" added Pam.

"She never talked to me about those things," answered Ms. Wiggins. "But I remember that she loved animals. For my birthdays she gave me little statues of ponies and horses. I still have them."

"I wonder how old Abigail was when she wrote the letter," said Lulu.

"We know that she wrote it in 1918," observed Anna.

"Do you know when she was born?" Pam

25

asked Ms. Wiggins. "We could figure out her age that way."

"Her birth date should be in the family Bible," said Ms. Wiggins. "There's a page where we write down every birth and death. I'm sure it goes back to Abigail's time."

Ms. Wiggins went to the bookshelves and took down a big black-and-gold Bible. She laid it on a table and opened it. "Let's see what we find," she said as she flipped a few pages. She stopped on a page of handwritten names and dates. Ms. Wiggins drew a finger along the list of names and stopped on one. "Here's my grandfather, John," she said. "And there's Abigail."

John Wiggins b. 1898 d. 1978
Abigail Wiggins b. 1908 d. 1972

"Abigail was born in 1908," said Pam. "So she was ten years old in 1918 when she wrote the letter."

"Just like us," said Anna softly.

Lulu imagined ten-year-old Abigail in the

parlor almost a hundred years earlier. What was it like to be a ten-year-old girl in 1918? she wondered.

"I wish we could find that sewing basket," said Pam. "Maybe the other letters are still in it."

"Do you think any of Abigail's things are still here?" asked Lulu.

Ms. Wiggins gently closed the Bible. "It's possible," she said. "I found my grandfather John's boyhood train set. It was in the attic in the garage. Abigail was his sister. Some of her girlhood things could be up there, too."

"Can we look?" asked Anna excitedly.

"Of course," said Ms. Wiggins.

The girls thanked Ms. Wiggins and went back outside. Lulu noticed Mike's and Tommy's bikes leaning against the barn. She didn't see the boys. Pam and Anna saw the bikes, too. Lulu motioned for Pam and Anna to follow her. The three girls sneaked into the garage through the back door.

Pam led the way up the stairs to the attic. Lulu followed. Anna hesitated. Lulu knew that Anna believed in ghosts. When Anna was five years old, she saw a ghost going out of her window. She showed Pam and Lulu the drawing she'd made of it.

"Don't worry, Anna," said Lulu. "If there are any ghosts in here, they're Ms. Wiggins's relatives. They'll be friendly ghosts."

"Good point," said Anna. She followed Pam and Lulu into the dark storage area.

Lulu looked around. Silhouettes of boxes and trunks filled the space. It was very dark and eerie. Maybe Anna's right, thought Lulu. Maybe there really are ghosts in here.

In the Dark

Lulu felt in the dark for a light switch. She found it, but no light came on. "The bulb's out," she announced. "We need a flashlight."

Anna grabbed Lulu's arm. "I heard something," she said.

"Oh-oo-oo," said Pam in a ghostly voice.

"Stop teasing," Anna told Pam. "I *did* hear something. Downstairs."

"Who's up there?" a voice shouted.

Anna let go of Lulu's arm. "It's Mike," she whispered.

The girls kept still and listened to the boys talking.

"Maybe it's the Pony Pests," said Tommy. "Their ponies are here."

The girls nudged one another in the dark. They silently agreed to play a trick on Mike and Tommy.

"Oh-oo-oo," said Pam in a spooky voice.

Lulu banged two boards together.

Anna made a high-pitched *ee-e-ee* sound.

"Did you hear that?" Mike asked Tommy. "Something weird is up there!"

"Do you think there's a ghost in the garage, buddy?" teased Tommy. "Is little Mikey afraid of ghosts?"

Mike must hate the way Tommy treats him, thought Lulu.

"I'm not afraid," said Mike. "It's just mice or squirrels, anyway. Come on. I have to tell Ms. Wiggins about the trees."

The girls didn't speak or move until the boys left the garage.

"Okay," whispered Pam. "They're gone."

"We might as well leave, too," said Lulu.

"It's too dark in here to look for Abigail's things."

"We can come back later," suggested Anna, "with flashlights."

"When Mike and Tommy aren't around," added Lulu.

The girls left the attic and sneaked out the back door of the garage. They saw Mike going into the house. Tommy was riding away on his bike.

"What do we do now?" asked Pam.

"I want to know more about the letter," said Anna.

"I have an idea," said Lulu. "Let's show it to Ms. McGee at the Wiggins Historical Society. I bet she can help us."

"She knows a lot about the old days in Wiggins," agreed Pam.

The three girls saddled up their ponies and rode to town. They put the ponies in the paddock behind Anna's house and gave them water. Next, they walked across the town green to the Wiggins Historical Society.

Janet McGee greeted them at the door. "What can I do for you girls?" she asked.

"We found a letter written in 1918," Pam told her.

"In a jar in a tree," added Anna. "We're the first ones to read it."

"How intriguing," said Janet McGee. "You can learn a lot about the past from old letters."

The girls followed Ms. McGee to her office. Lulu gave her the letter. "AW stands for Abigail Wiggins," Lulu told her.

Ms. McGee sat at the desk and carefully read the letter. When she finished, she looked up at the girls. "It's amazing that you found this," she said.

"Why would someone leave a letter in a tree, though?" asked Anna. "Did people do that in 1918?"

"It's the first time I've heard of it," answered Ms. McGee. "But not everyone had telephones back then."

"I wonder what life was like in 1918," said Lulu.

"There was a lot going on in Wiggins that year," answered Ms. McGee. "Why don't you look at issues of the *Wiggins Gazette* from 1918? I think you'd find it very interesting. We have those old newspapers on microfilm."

In a few minutes, the girls were sitting in a small circle around the microfilm reader. Pam scrolled until she found October of 1918. Then she slowed down so they could read the articles.

"In 1918 there was a world war," commented Pam. "World War I."

"The women's club was making bandages for the soldiers," Lulu noticed.

"And knitting socks for them," Anna added.

"Here's the first page for October 15, 1918," said Pam. She stopped on page one.

"There was an influenza epidemic," exclaimed Lulu.

"What's influenza?" asked Anna.

"It's another name for the flu," said Pam.

Lulu read the lead article out loud.

TUESDAY, OCTOBER 15, 1918

INFLUENZA EPIDEMIC HITS WIGGINS

The townspeople of Wiggins are suffering mightily from the influenza epidemic. There were ten deaths this week. Five people died of the influenza the previous week. Friends and neighbors, please stay away from public places and one another. This influenza is highly contagious. All schools are closed until further notice. The public library and movie theater are closed, as well.

"I had the flu last year," said Anna. "A lot of kids in our class had it. But they didn't close school."

Lulu silently read the rest of the article. "People got pneumonia from this flu," she told Anna. "They died from it."

"I bet they didn't have antibiotics in 1918," said Pam, "or a lot of the medicines we have today."

"Abigail probably had influenza when she wrote the letter," said Pam. "That's why LS couldn't visit her."

"Because she might catch it," concluded Lulu.

"Maybe she caught it, anyway," said Anna. "Maybe that's why LS never got the letter." Tears came into Anna's eyes. "Because she died."

Lulu put an arm around Anna's shoulder.

Pam turned off the microfilm reader and rolled the film back.

"I wish we knew who LS was," she said. "I wish we at least knew her name."

The three girls went back to Janet McGee's office and told her what they had learned.

"How do we find out who LS was?" Pam asked Ms. McGee.

"Do you have any idea when she was born?" Ms. McGee asked.

"Abigail, her best friend, was born in 1908," answered Lulu. "So LS was probably born right around then."

"We have lists of people born in Wiggins for each year," said Ms. McGee. "But I don't have those records. They are at the town hall."

"We could look for someone with the initials LS," suggested Lulu.

"Milton Shapiro is the town clerk," Ms. McGee told them. "He'll help you." She looked at her watch. "If you go to town hall now, you'll catch him before lunch."

The girls thanked Janet McGee and ran across the town green.

Lulu suddenly stopped.

"What's wrong?" asked Pam.

"Maybe LS wasn't born in Wiggins," said Lulu. "Like me. I live in Wiggins, but I wasn't born here."

"I hope LS was born here," said Pam. "We *have* to find out more about her. There might be other clues in the town records."

"Like when she died," said Anna. "I'm so afraid she died of the influenza."

Me, too, thought Lulu. Me, too.

Peek into the Past

The Pony Pals went into the town hall. The town clerk's office was in the back. Mr. Shapiro was sitting at a library table reading a huge book. More books lined the shelves on the wall behind him. He looked up when the girls came in.

The Pony Pals introduced themselves and told Mr. Shapiro about the letter.

"Can we see a list of the people born in Wiggins in 1908?" asked Pam.

"Certainly," answered Mr. Shapiro.

He looked over the shelves of books,

pulled one out, and opened it on the table. The girls stood around him.

"Here's 1908," he said, pointing to the top of a page. "Fifty-one people were born in Wiggins that year. They're listed by date of birth, starting in January."

Lulu looked down the list of names: EMMA OLSON, CHARLES LINER, EDWIN COOK.

"Here's one with the initials LS," said Anna. She pointed to a name. "Lawrence Sanders. A boy."

"Lawrence *Sanders*," said Lulu. "I wonder if he's related to me."

"You should ask your grandmother," said Anna.

"Here's a girl whose initials are LS," exclaimed Pam. "Lydia Simpson."

Lulu studied the entry for Lydia Simpson.

Aug. 3 Simpson, Lydia F.

The girls checked the other births for 1908. Lydia Simpson was the only female with the initials LS.

"It tells you a lot about her," said Lulu. "Her parents' names, where they were born, how old they were."

"Does it say when Lydia died?" asked Anna.

"No," answered Pam.

"The woman you're looking for could still be alive," Mr. Shapiro told the girls. "There's a Lydia at the nursing home on School Street. She was my fifth-grade teacher."

"What was your teacher's last name?" asked Lulu.

"Eastman," answered Mr. Shapiro. "Lydia Eastman. But Eastman was her married name. I don't know her maiden name."

"Maybe it began with S," said Lulu excitedly.

"Mrs. Eastman loved to teach us the history of Wiggins," said Mr. Shapiro. "She told us about the influenza epidemic of 1918. She said that she was a young girl at the time."

Pam pointed to Lydia Simpson's name in the book. "This Lydia would have been ten years old in 1918."

"Maybe the Lydia in the nursing home is LS," said Anna. "The girl Abigail wrote to."

"Even if she isn't the right Lydia," said Lulu, "she might know who LS was."

"And Abigail Wiggins," added Pam. "They were all the same age."

"Why don't you visit Lydia Eastman?" suggested Mr. Shapiro. "She's at the Good View Nursing Home."

The girls thanked Mr. Shapiro and left.

"Should we go to the nursing home now?" asked Anna as they walked outside.

Lulu looked up at the big clock on the town hall. It was twelve twenty-five. "It's lunchtime," she said.

"Maybe we should go a little later," said Pam.

"Let's go to my house," suggested Lulu. "We can make macaroni and cheese. After lunch, we'll go visit Lydia."

"We can ask your grandmother if you're related to Lawrence Sanders," added Pam.

The girls went down the block to Lulu's house. Grandmother Sanders was in the dining room eating a sandwich. Lulu asked her about Lawrence Sanders.

Grandmother Sanders smiled. "He was your great-grandfather on your father's side," she answered. "Lawrence was my father."

A little chill ran through Lulu. She'd seen the record of her great-grandfather's birth. He was born the same year as Abigail. He probably knew her and Lydia.

After lunch, the girls gave apples to their ponies. "We're working on a mystery, Snow White," Lulu told her pony, "thanks to you."

Snow White nodded as if she understood. Lulu hugged her.

"Let's bring Lydia a present," said Pam.

"Flowers would be nice," suggested Anna.

Lulu and Pam agreed that flowers were a perfect gift for Lydia.

"And we'll show her the letter," added Lulu. "Even if she isn't the right Lydia."

The Pony Pals pooled their money and bought a bouquet of flowers at the Green Market.

At two o'clock, the three girls walked into the Good View Nursing Home. A receptionist was at the front desk.

"We're here to visit Lydia Eastman," Pam told the receptionist.

"Are you related to Mrs. Eastman?" she asked.

"No," answered Pam.

The Pony Pals exchanged a glance. What if the receptionist wouldn't let them visit Lydia?

"We want to ask her some questions about the past," explained Lulu. "About when she was a girl."

The receptionist smiled. "Lydia would like that. She loves to talk about the past," she said. She pointed down a long corridor. "She's in room 102. Don't stay too long. She tires easily."

The girls walked down the corridor. They passed an elderly man using a walker. Lulu smiled and said hi to him. The man smiled back at her.

The door to room 102 was open. A white-haired woman sat in a wheelchair. She was reading. Lulu knocked lightly on the open door. The woman looked up. When she saw the girls, she closed her book and smiled.

"Come in," she said.

The girls walked over to Lydia and introduced themselves. Anna gave her the flowers.

"We'd like to ask you some questions about life in Wiggins in 1918," said Lulu.

"Is it for a school project?" asked Lydia Eastman.

"It's just for ourselves," answered Lulu.

Lulu told Lydia how they had found the letter. Anna showed it to her.

Lydia read the letter. Then she turned from the girls and looked out the window. Everyone was silent for a few seconds.

"We wondered what your last name was," said Lulu softly. "Before you married Mr. Eastman."

Lydia finally looked back at them. She had tears in her eyes. "My name was Lydia Simpson," she said. "This letter was written to me."

Evidence on the Bureau

Lydia smiled at the three girls. "Thank you for bringing this letter to me. Please sit down."

Pam and Lulu sat on the edge of the bed. Anna sat in the chair near Lydia's wheelchair.

"Abigail Wiggins and I were best friends," Lydia told them. She held up the letter. "Didn't she have lovely handwriting? And look at her wonderful drawing."

"I love that drawing," said Anna.

"Why did you leave letters in a tree?" asked Lulu.

"That tree was halfway between our houses," answered Lydia. "Abigail and I only used it for letters during the influenza epidemic. The influenza was very catching, you know. I caught it, anyway. Almost everyone in Wiggins had that flu."

"Is that why you didn't pick up this letter?" asked Pam. "Because you were sick?"

"That's right," answered Lydia.

"Why didn't you get it when you were better?" asked Pam.

"I guess I never knew it was there," said Lydia. "It was a sad, sad winter. My baby brother, Mike, died in that epidemic. And so many others."

Anna put a hand on Lydia's arm. "I'm sorry," she said softly.

Lydia patted Anna's hand. "Thank you, dear," she said.

No one said anything for a few seconds.

Lydia broke the silence. "The summer after the epidemic, Abigail and I were together almost every day," she said. "We helped each other with chores and rode our ponies." She smiled to herself. "We didn't need the letter tree."

"You and Abigail were Pony Pals," said Lulu.

"That's right, dear," said Lydia. "We were Pony Pals."

She looked down at the bunch of roses on her lap. "These are so lovely. Roses are my favorite flowers." Lydia pointed to the bureau. "There's a vase on the bureau. Could one of you fill it with water? We'll give the flowers a drink."

"I'll do it," said Lulu.

She went over to the bureau. The vase was behind a row of framed photos. As Lulu reached for the vase, she glanced at the photos. She was shocked by what she saw. There was a photo of Mike Lacey with his sister, Rosalie. The picture beside that was of Mrs. Lacey. The next one was Mike's school picture.

"You have a lot of pictures," Lulu told Lydia.

"Oh, yes," said Lydia as she wheeled herself over to the bureau. "They're all of my family."

Lulu motioned for Pam and Anna to come over, too.

Anna's mouth dropped open when she saw the pictures of Mike and his family. Pam's eyes opened wide in surprise.

Lydia picked up the photo of Mike and Rosalie. "Those are my great-grandchildren," she said. "Mike and Rosalie. Their mother is my granddaughter. I am very blessed to have them close by. Mike comes by here every week. He's a wonderful boy." She smiled at the girls. "You would like him."

The Pony Pals exchanged a glance and silently agreed that they wouldn't tell Lydia that they already knew Mike.

Lulu filled the vase with water and arranged the roses. Pam and Anna sat on the bed facing Lydia.

"We'd love to hear about your pony, Bangles," Pam told Lydia.

"And that special riding field," added Anna.

"Bangles was a Shetland pony," said Lydia. "He was a stubborn animal, but very, very smart."

"Just like my pony, Acorn," said Anna.

Lulu put the vase of flowers on the bureau. "What was Wildflower like?" she asked as she sat in the chair.

"Wildflower had a very sweet temperament," answered Lydia. "She was a marvelous worker in the fields. Bangles was a good worker, too. He was the milk-cart pony. My father sold milk from our cows door-to-door."

"Your ponies had to work?" asked Lulu with surprise.

"Oh, yes," answered Lydia. "There weren't a lot of tractors in those days. And not many cars or trucks. Not in Wiggins, anyway. We children worked hard, too. At ten years of age I was making cheese, baking bread, canning food for winter. Oh, we had many chores."

"I thought you rode your ponies for fun," said Anna. "Like we do."

Lydia smiled. "We did that, too," she said. "Mostly on Sundays. Abigail and I had our secret riding field, way up behind her house. There was a view of Lake Appamapog. My, it was lovely." Lydia closed her eyes. No one spoke. Lydia's eyes remained closed.

Pam tugged on Lulu's sleeve. "I think she's asleep," she whispered.

Lydia slowly opened her eyes. "I was just remembering those wonderful afternoons of riding," she said. "We were free in that field. Free from chores and worries." She sighed. "But I *am* a little tired. Would you girls come back and visit me again?"

"Yes," said the Pony Pals in unison as they stood up to leave.

"That would be lovely," said Lydia as she closed her eyes again.

"Bye," whispered Pam.

"We'll see you soon," said Lulu.

"Thank you," added Anna in a hushed voice.

Then they tiptoed out of Lydia's room.

When they were on the street again, the Pony Pals grinned excitedly at one another.

"We did it!" shouted Lulu. "We found LS."

"She was alive all this time!" said Pam.

"She's so *nice*," said Anna.

"And she's Mike Lacey's great-grand-mother!" added Lulu.

"That's not *her* fault," said Anna.

They broke out laughing and walked to-ward Anna's.

"I can't wait to tell Ms. Wiggins who LS is," said Pam.

"Do we have to tell Mike?" asked Lulu.

"The letter was written to his great-grandmother," said Pam. "I guess we'll have to tell him eventually."

Pam looked at her watch. "I've got to do barn chores," she said.

"What time is it?" asked Anna.

"Two-thirty," answered Pam.

"I have my tutor at three," Anna said.

"And I need to do a book report for English," added Lulu.

By the time the Pony Pals reached Anna's house, they had a plan. They'd meet the next morning at the three birch trees on Pony Pal Trail. From there, they'd go together to Ms. Wiggins's. In the afternoon, they'd visit Lydia again.

Anna and Lulu helped Pam saddle up Lightning. "Let's all bring flashlights to Ms. Wiggins's," Lulu told her friends. "We'll search that attic for Abigail's sewing basket."

"I wish Lydia had told us exactly where the special field is," said Anna.

"We can ask her tomorrow," said Pam.

Lulu couldn't wait for tomorrow to come.

The Garden Visit

The next morning, the Pony Pals rode over to Ms. Wiggins's. She was near the barn grooming Picasso. The girls dismounted and tied their ponies to the hitching post. Snow White whinnied a hello to Picasso. The big black horse nodded and whinnied back.

"You girls disappeared yesterday," said Ms. Wiggins. "I looked for you in the attic, but you were gone."

"The lights didn't work," explained Pam.

"Sorry we didn't say good-bye," added Anna.

"I noticed that the lights in the attic were out," said Ms. Wiggins. "I had Mike replace the bulbs. There's plenty of light up there now."

Anna and Lulu exchanged a glance. They both wondered the same thing. Was Mike afraid when he went into the dark attic? Did he really think he had heard a ghost?

Pam picked up a brush and helped groom Picasso. The big black horse nickered contentedly. He loved attention.

"Did you learn any more about my great-aunt Abigail and LS?" asked Ms. Wiggins.

Pam told Ms. Wiggins about going to the Wiggins Historical Society. Anna explained how they found LS in the birth records at town hall. They all talked about visiting Lydia Simpson Eastman at the nursing home.

"Lydia is Mike Lacey's great-grandmother," said Lulu.

"She has a lot of pictures of him," said Anna.

"That's so amazing!" exclaimed Ms. Wiggins. "My great-aunt and Mike's great-grandmother were best friends. Have you told Mike?"

"Not yet," admitted Anna.

"The letter can't be kept secret from him anymore," said Ms. Wiggins. "It was written to his great-grandmother."

"We know," said Lulu. She scratched Picasso's forehead. "Did you tell Mike we were in the attic yesterday?"

"Yes," Ms. Wiggins answered. "But I didn't tell him what you were looking for. Mike's working in the vegetable garden this morning. You can tell him all about the letter."

"Okay," agreed Pam. "But first we'll put our ponies in the paddock."

"I'm taking Picasso out for a trail ride," Ms. Wiggins told them. "Good luck in your search."

The Pony Pals led their ponies around to the paddock. Lulu noticed a mountain bike leaning against a tree. "Tommy Rand is here," she told Anna and Pam.

"Do we *have* to tell Mike now?" asked Anna. "I hate the way he acts when Tommy is around."

"Ms. Wiggins sort of told us to," said Lulu.

"I'll put our ponies in the paddock," offered Pam. "You two can talk to Mike."

Anna rolled her eyes. "Thanks a lot," she said.

Lulu and Anna went around the house to the vegetable garden. Mike was turning over the soil with a shovel. Tommy leaned on the gate doing nothing.

"Hey, here come the Pony Pests," said Tommy. "Quick! Call the exterminator."

Anna and Lulu ignored Tommy.

Lulu told Mike how they found the letter and that Ms. Wiggins's great-aunt wrote it.

Anna told him that the letter was written to his great-grandmother.

"Wow, Granny's going to love that," exclaimed Mike. "She's still alive, you know."

"We know," said Anna and Lulu together.

"We already told her about it," said Lulu.

"And we gave her the letter," added Anna.

"I wonder if there are any more letters," said Mike.

"We wondered the same thing," said Anna. "There weren't any more in the tree. The letter said Abigail kept the letters your great-grandmother wrote to her. She kept them in her sewing basket."

"Is that why you were in the garage yesterday?" asked Mike. "Were you looking for Abigail's sewing basket?"

"Sewing basket?!" Tommy laughed. "What do you care about sewing baskets, Mike? Old letters and old ladies! Bor-ing."

Mike swung around to face Tommy. "The *old lady* is my great-grandmother," he said. "And she isn't boring."

"Ex-cuse me," said Tommy in a mocking voice. "Well, I've got more important stuff to do than talk about old bor-ing stuff."

"Good riddance," said Anna.

Mike suddenly turned to Anna and Lulu. "You guys are *bugging* me," he said. He called after Tommy. "Get it? The Pony *Pests* are *bugging* me. Ha-ha."

But Tommy didn't laugh. He didn't even turn around, but walked away.

"Why do you let Tommy treat you like that?" Lulu asked Mike.

"He's a lousy friend," added Anna.

"It's none of your business," Mike told them.

"Well, ex-cuse me," said Lulu.

Anna and Lulu left the garden and met Pam in the garage. They all went up to the attic over the garage.

Lulu opened the door, felt for the light switch, and flipped it on. She looked around. The space was crammed with boxes, trunks, and old furniture.

"There's so much stuff," exclaimed Anna. "How are we going to look at all of it?"

"Let's each take a pile," suggested Lulu.

"Good idea," agreed Anna.

Lulu started with a big box. It was filled with old hats. She put on a pink hat with a black veil. "How do I look?" she asked.

"You look beau-ti-ful, darling," said Anna in a fancy actress voice.

Pam and Anna put on hats, too.

"We're detectives with style," teased Anna.

The girls kept the hats on while they continued their search.

Lulu opened another box. It was crammed with old books. She opened another box. More books.

"There's an old trunk here," Pam announced. "But I can't open it."

Lulu went over to the trunk. She felt all around the lock. Her finger rubbed against a small latch. "I think I've got it," she said. Lulu pressed the latch with her finger and the lock released.

Pam opened the trunk.

"What did you find?" asked Anna.

Lulu motioned for her to come over.

The Pony Pals peered into the trunk. A pile of books was stacked on one side. A sock doll and wooden toys filled the rest of the space.

"Maybe it's Abigail's trunk," said Anna.

Pam picked up a book and opened it. She pointed to the bookplate on the front page:

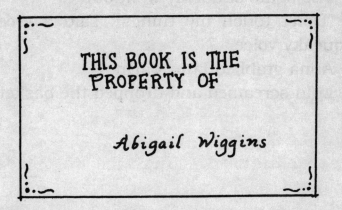

THIS BOOK IS THE PROPERTY OF

Abigail Wiggins

"It *is* Abigail's trunk," said Lulu.

"It's like she's here with us," whispered Anna.

"Like a ghost?" asked Lulu.

Anna nodded.

Lulu took out the toys and sock doll. A yellow straw basket was under them. Anna reached into the trunk and removed the top of the basket.

The Pony Pals looked down on scraps of cloth and spools of thread.

Lulu slowly lifted the basket out of the trunk. Are the letters Lydia wrote to Abigail in here? she wondered.

The lights suddenly went out.

"Don't touch my things," said a creepy, squeaky voice.

Anna grabbed Lulu's arm.

Lulu screamed and dropped the basket.

The Top Hat

"**W**ho said that?" whispered Pam.

The lights went back on. Lulu heard some-one running down the stairs. She ran to the door and saw Tommy Rand running out of the garage.

"You creep!" Lulu shouted after him.

"It wasn't my idea," said a voice behind Lulu.

Lulu turned and faced Mike Lacey. "But you were with him!" she shouted.

"Get out of here," ordered Pam.

"You're looking for my granny's letters,"

said Mike. "I want to see them, too. Besides, you tried to scare us yesterday."

"Did we really scare you?" asked Anna.

"Sort of," admitted Mike.

Lulu looked out the window. "Tommy's leaving," she announced. "The coward."

"You found a sewing basket," said Mike. "I saw."

"You were spying on us!" accused Pam.

"Just for a minute," explained Mike. He smiled. "I didn't see you put on those funny hats."

"If you want to help us you have to wear an old hat, too," challenged Anna.

Lulu took a man's top hat out of the box and handed it to Mike.

He put it on.

Pam and Lulu exchanged a glance. They were surprised that Mike was being such a good sport.

"You look like the Ringmaster at the circus, Mike," commented Anna.

"Now let's see what's in Abigail's sewing basket," Mike said.

Lulu picked up the sewing basket. The others gathered around her. Anna took out the sewing things. There weren't any letters on the bottom.

"They're not here," said Anna sadly.

Mike looked around the storage room. "Let's keep looking," he said. "Maybe there's another sewing basket."

"Wait a minute," said Lulu. She turned the basket upside down and shook it. The bottom made a fluttery sound. "It think it has a false bottom," she told the others. Lulu took the scissors from Anna. She pried out the cardboard bottom of the basket. It came up easily.

"It *was* a false bottom," said Pam.

Lulu held up three envelopes tied with a pink ribbon. She carefully untied the ribbon. All the envelopes had been opened and contained letters. "For AW," was written on each one.

"My granny will be so happy," said Mike.

I'm happy, too, thought Lulu. She couldn't wait to read the letters that Lydia had written to Abigail in 1918.

The Pony Pals and Mike sat on boxes and Lulu pulled out the first letter. She handed it to Pam. Pam read it out loud.

October 1, 1918

Dear A W,

I hope you are feeling better. Mother wouldn't allow me to go to church today. She said I might catch the influenza there. I prayed at home. I prayed for you to be better soon and for our soldiers in the war, especially my father.

I wish I could take care of you. I would wipe your forehead with cool water and read you stories.

Did you know that the schools are closed? I am very busy all day long. I have many chores to do. Our farmhand has the influenza, so Mother and I milk the cows. I also take care of my baby brother, so

*Mother can do other farm
chores. I don't mind taking
care of Mike. He is so darling.
Today he said my name for
the first time. He calls me
Leeda.
I will put this letter in the
tree before I do the milking
and feed Bangles. I'll give
Bangles a kiss for you.*

*your best friend,
L S*

"Mike is Lydia's baby brother who died," said Anna.

"She told me about that," said Mike softly. "I'm named after him."

Lulu took out the next letter and handed it to Mike. "You read this one," she said.

October 6, 1918

*Dear A W,
There's a new law in
Wiggins. If you go out, you
have to wear a white cotton*

70

mask over your nose and mouth. It looks very strange. I don't go to town, anyway. I'm too busy at home. Last night I dreamt about our special field. We were riding with three other girls and their ponies. It was so beautiful. We were all best friends, Pony Friends. Around and around we rode. We were free. Free of war. Free of influenza. Free of chores.

George O. is helping my mother in the fields today. Mother thinks he's a "nice boy." I told her that he's not so nice when he's with Edwin P.

Your last letter was long, so I think you are getting better.

Your best friend in the world,
LS

Mike folded the letter carefully, put it in the envelope, and handed it back to Lulu.

"George O. sounds like you, Mike," said Pam.

"And Edwin P. is like Tommy," added Anna.

Mike made a nervous cough. "Yeah, yeah, yeah," he said.

"There's one more letter," said Lulu.

"You read it," said Mike.

Lulu pulled out the letter and read it out loud.

October 14, 1918

Dear AW:
I'm sorry that I didn't write for so many days. I have been very busy. There is so much to do. Even Mother was sick, though now she is better. I think Mike has a fever. Mother is rocking him. She

*is crying. We are so afraid
he has the influenza. I am
crying, too.*

   Pray for Mike.

     Your best friend,

       LS

Postscript

 *If I get sick who will
help Mother take care of
Mike ?*

"That's a sad letter," said Anna.

"Because we know that baby Mike died," added Lulu.

Lulu looked over at Mike. She held out the letters. "Do you want to give these to your great-grandmother?" she asked.

"You found them," he said. "So you should give them to her. I have to finish digging the garden." He took off the top hat and handed it to Lulu. Then he left.

Lulu went to the window. She watched Mike walking slowly back to the garden. The letters made him sad, she thought. Baby Mike was his great-uncle.

"Let's bring the letters to Lydia now," suggested Pam.

Lulu and Anna agreed.

Lulu put the hats back in the box. Pam packed Abigail's trunk. Anna put the letters in order and tied them with the pink ribbon.

"We'll ask Lydia where that special riding field is," said Anna.

"I hope she hasn't forgotten how to get there," said Pam.

"Do you remember Lydia's dream?" asked Lulu. "The one she wrote about in the letter?"

"She and Abigail were riding with three other girls and their ponies," said Pam.

"Three girls like us," said Lulu.

"I want to ride in that field," said Anna. "I want to make Lydia's dream come true." She looked up at Lulu and Pam. "Do you?"

Pam nodded.

"Me, too," said Lulu.

Family Photos

An hour later, the girls walked into the Good View Nursing Home. The receptionist recognized them. "Mrs. Eastman was hoping you'd come today," she said. "She has something to show you."

"We have something to show her, too," said Anna.

Lydia was sitting by the window. A photo album lay open on her lap. She smiled brightly when she saw the Pony Pals. "I found some photos," she told them. "Of Abby and me."

The girls stood around Lydia. She pointed to a black-and-white photo of two girls, arm in arm, smiling. "That's us," she said. "We were at the county fair."

Anna pointed to another photo on the page. It was of a young girl holding a baby. "Is that baby Mike?" she asked softly.

"Yes," answered Lydia. "It is. That's me holding him." She looked up at Anna. "When I was your age."

Lydia turned back a page and pointed to another photo. "Look at this one," she said. "It's the only photo I have of my dear old Bangles. Abigail and Wildflower are with us."

"You and Abigail look so happy," said Anna.

"We were," said Lydia. "And wasn't that Wildflower a beauty?"

Lulu studied the photo.

"It's a wonderful picture," said Pam.

"We found the letters you wrote to Abigail," Anna told Lydia.

Lulu handed Lydia the three envelopes

tied with pink ribbon. "Mike helped us look for them," she said.

"Such a nice boy," said Lydia.

Sometimes he *is* nice, thought Lulu.

"We already read the letters," Pam told her. "Mike, too. I hope you don't mind."

"I'm glad you did," said Lydia.

Lydia put the letters in her photo album and closed it. "I'll read them later," she said. "When I'm alone."

"We have a question to ask you," said Anna.

"Do you remember how to get to your special riding field?" asked Pam.

"We'd like to ride there," explained Lulu. "If you don't mind."

"Of course I don't mind," said Lydia. "I would like it very much."

"Can you tell us how to get there?" asked Pam. "Anna can draw a map."

Anna took out her sketch pad and pencil.

"Where will you be starting from?" asked Lydia.

"Where did you and Abigail start from?" asked Anna.

Lydia looked out the window and thought. "We started in the big field behind the barn," she said.

"That's where we'll start then," said Lulu.

Lydia reached for Anna's pad and pencil. "I'll draw the map," she said.

Lydia drew a barn and the field. Then she added hills and trails to the west and north of the barn and field. "There was a big boulder far up on the trail," she said. "That rock was as big as a girl on a pony." She drew the boulder. "That's where we turned right onto another trail. We rode on that second trail for a little way. When we came to a row of trees, we were there." Lydia added a row of trees to her map. Then she handed the pad back to Anna.

The Pony Pals studied the map.

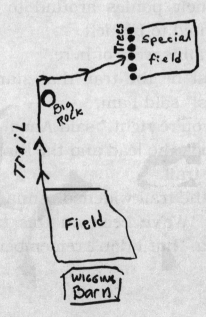

"It might not be a field anymore," said Lulu. "Trees could have grown up."

"I just hope we can find it," said Anna.

Lydia smiled at her. "I hope you do, too," she said. "And I hope that you can ride there."

After lunch, the girls rode back to Ms. Wiggins's.

They went directly to the field behind the barn. Lulu looked at the map. "We should face north," she said. The three riders turned their ponies around to face north. Lulu pointed to her left.

"The trail is west of here."

"It must be the trail that starts near the pine trees," said Pam.

"I bet you're right," said Anna.

Lulu took the lead and the three riders entered the trail.

When the trail widened, Anna rode up beside her. "We've been on this trail before," said Anna, "but I don't remember a big boulder."

"We weren't looking for it before," said Lulu.

A few minutes later, Lulu halted Snow White and pointed into the woods to their right. "There's a big boulder," she said.

Anna dismounted and went behind the boulder. "There's a trail here," she said. "A nice wide one."

The girls led their ponies around the boulder and onto a wide trail. They rode until they came to an even row of trees.

"The field should be behind the trees," said Pam.

They all dismounted and led their ponies into the field. The grass was high and there was a lot of brush.

"Abigail's and Lydia's special field is all grown over," observed Lulu sadly.

"It's not safe for riding," concluded Pam.

"We can mow it down," said a male voice.

The Pony Pals saw Mike. He was sitting in the grass next to his mountain bike.

Lulu and Pam exchanged a glance. They had wanted to keep the field a secret from Mike and Tommy.

"What are you doing here?" Lulu asked Mike.

"I come here a lot," he answered.

"With Tommy?" asked Pam.

"Tommy doesn't know about it," said Mike. "I come when I want to be alone."

"Don't worry, we won't tell him," said Lulu. She smiled at Mike. "We don't want him to know about it, either."

Lulu looked at the overgrown field. "Did your granny tell you about it before?" she asked. "Is that how you found it?"

"No," he said. "I've been coming here for a long time. I didn't know she came here, too."

That's so spooky, thought Lulu. Mike and his great-grandmother picked out the same special place.

"We wanted to ride here," explained Pam. "Just like Abigail and Lydia."

"Granny told me," said Mike. He looked around. "We can mow the field and clear out some of the bushes. I'll ask Ms. Wiggins. Mr. Silver can come up with the tractor."

"We'll help," said Lulu.

"Let's get started," said Pam. "There's a lot of work to do."

The girls and Mike rode back to Ms. Wiggins's.

Ms. Wiggins loved the idea of clearing the old field. The three girls, Mr. Silver, and Mike worked there until it was dark. The ponies helped by eating some of the grass.

That night, the Pony Pals had a barn sleepover in the Crandals' hayloft. Their sleeping bags were laid out in a row, facing the open loft door.

Lulu looked out at the stars. "I can't wait to ride in that field tomorrow," she said. "I'm going to think about Abigail and Lydia riding there."

"Maybe the spirit of Abigail and the two ponies will ride with us," said Anna.

"Are you afraid to ride there?" asked Pam.

"No," said Anna. "I'm not afraid of *those* ghosts."

Neither am I, thought Lulu.

Rider from the Past

After breakfast the next morning, the Pony Pals prepared their ponies for the special ride. Pam rubbed oil on the marking on Lightning's forehead. The white upside-down heart glistened in the sunlight. Anna put a row of little bells on Acorn's bridle. Lulu braided blue ribbons into Snow White's mane.

The girls mounted their ponies and rode to the field behind Ms. Wiggins's barn. Ms. Wiggins was standing next to the barn. She was putting the cart harness on Beauty. The Pony Pals waved to her.

Ms. Wiggins smiled and waved back. "Have a wonderful ride," she called.

"We will," Anna yelled back.

The girls rode onto the trail that led north to the boulder. Mr. Silver had mowed a wide path around the boulder. They followed it onto the next trail. Finally, they came to the freshly mowed field. It was perfect for riding.

"Remember what Lydia wrote in the letter," said Pam. " *'Last night I dreamt about our special field. We were riding with three other girls and their ponies.'* "

" *'It was so beautiful,'* " continued Lulu. " *'We were all best friends, Pony Friends. Around and around we rode. We were free.'* "

"I hope Abigail's spirit rides with us today," whispered Anna.

"You take the lead, Lulu," said Pam, "because Snow White found the letter."

The three friends lined up to begin their special ride.

"Listen," said Lulu. "Someone's coming."

Anna's eyes opened wide. "Maybe it's Abigail, Wildflower, and Bangles," she whispered.

But it wasn't ponies from the past that rode into the field. It was Mike Lacey on his mountain bike. Lulu didn't feel angry with Mike for coming to the field. It was his special place. And his great-grandmother's.

"Hi," he said with a big grin. "I have a surprise for you."

"What?" asked Anna.

Ms. Wiggins drove her pony cart into the field. Lydia sat in the seat beside her. Lydia waved to the Pony Pals.

The girls hollered hello, as they rode their ponies over to meet Ms. Wiggins and Lydia.

Lydia looked around the field. "How wonderful!" she exclaimed. "I can't believe I'm back here." She patted Mike on the arm. "It was Mike's idea." She smiled at the Pony Pals. "These must be the ponies you told me about."

Acorn did his bowing trick for Lydia. She rubbed Lightning's lucky heart marking.

Snow White lowered her head and Lydia patted her.

"Now will you ride for me?" asked Lydia.

"Sure," said Lulu.

"We'd love to," added Anna.

The three girls rode around the field. As they rode, Lulu heard the hoofbeats of a pony passing. Snow White turned and nodded, as if to another pony. Lulu looked to see if it was Anna or Pam passing them. But she saw no one. She turned in her saddle. Pam and Anna were still behind her. She looked ahead. No one, that she could see, had passed her and Snow White. A shiver ran through Lulu. A happy shiver. The spirit of Abigail was riding with them.

Ms. Wiggins drove the pony cart up behind Anna and Acorn. Mike came behind them on his bike.

Lydia is riding in her special field again, thought Lulu.

The parade of ponies, pony cart, and bike made two turns around the field.

When they stopped, Lydia was smiling

through joyful tears. "How wonderful," she said. "I've lived the dream I had when I was ten."

No one spoke. They all looked out at the sunlit field.

Lulu leaned over and put her arms around Snow White's neck. "Thank you," she whispered in her pony's ear. "Thank you for leading us to the past."

Dear Reader,

I am having fun researching and writing the Pony Pal books. I've met great kids and wonderful ponies at homes, farms, and riding schools. Some of my ideas for Pony Pal adventures have even come from these visits.

I remember the day I made up the main characters for the series. I was walking on a country road in New England. First, I decided that the three girls would be smart, independent, and kind. Then I gave them their names—Pam, Anna, and Lulu. (Look at the initial of each girl's name. See what it spells when you put them together.) Later, I created the three ponies. When I reached home, I turned on my computer and started to write. And I haven't stopped since!

My friends say that I am a little bit like all of the Pony Pals. I am very organized, like Pam. I love nature, like Lulu. But I think that I am most like Anna. I am dyslexic and a good artist, just like her.

Readers often wonder about my life. I live in an apartment in New York City near Central Park and the Museum of Natural History. I enjoy swimming, hiking, painting, and reading. I also love to make up stories. I have been writing novels for children and young adults for more than twenty years! Several of my books have won the Children's Choice Award.

Many Pony Pal readers send me letters, drawings, and photos. I tape them to the wall in my office. They inspire me to write more Pony Pal stories. Thank you very much!

I don't ride anymore and I've never had a pony. But you don't have to ride to love ponies! And you certainly don't need a pony to be a Pony Pal.

Happy Reading,

Jeanne Betancourt

Pony Pals®

Be a Pony Pal®!

Available wherever you buy books, or use this order form.